Julie

At the Farm

Illustrations: Jan Ivens

Text: Mireille Van Wilderode

Translation: Hélène Morin

On a sunny summer day Julie and her faithful dog Boy are walking across fields to Mr. Munch's farm. Julie's mother asked them to get some fresh eggs. Along the way they say hello to a few cows peacefully grazing the soft grass. Julie is glad to go to the farm because there is always something going on there.

Julie sees Mr. Munch working on his tractor's engine. "Hello Mr. Munch! What are you doing?" she asks. Mr. Munch mumbles as he straightens up, his hands black with grease. "Well, little Julie... I'm trying to repair that stupid tractor!" "May I help you?" Julie says. "I'm afraid not, even though I could use some help."

"My mother wants some eggs," announces Julie. "May I pick them myself?"
"Good idea! That way, I can finish repairing my tractor!" answers Mr. Munch.

And the farmer dives again under the hood of his tractor.

"Come on, Boy. Let's got to the henhouse. We'll bring Mom something to make a delicious omelet. Yummy!" exclaims Julie as she walks towards the farmyard.

A flock of hens and their chicks are picking grains of corn from the ground. "Here we come..." says Julie softly as she opens the gate slowly and carefully. But Boy manages to slip in before her and runs into the yard barking.

The big dog's entrance scatters the hens in a panic. The little creatures start running in all directions, cackling and clucking. What a mess!

"No, don't!" cries out Julie, suddenly worried. "Come back immediately, Boy. Heel!" But Boy isn't listening at all, he's having great fun!

Reluctantly, Boy finally comes back to Julie's side. A good dog must always obey his mistress! Julie scolds him: "What have you done! We came to pick some eggs, not to chase those poor hens! Look at the little darlings, you scared them to death... Don't be surprised if they don't want to play with you in the future. You acted like a silly puppy with no manners. Now lie down, and don't move!"

Boy is ashamed of himself. He settles down quietly and watches Julie. She's looking for eggs in every nook and cranny of the henhouse.
She takes the nicest and the biggest ones.

Once in a while, she nudges a hen softly to take her egg.

"Obviously, she knows how to do this much better than I do, "thinks Boy, who would like to make up for his behavior.

Suddenly, he sees an egg that Julie forgot. He takes it between his teeth and runs to his mistress, but the egg breaks. Julie starts laughing. "Poor Boy! You see, you can't make an omelet without breaking eggs!"

Julie decides it is time to go see Mr. Munch. "Did you find enough eggs?" he asks. "It's certainly enough. We'll be able to make a giant omelet and maybe some pancakes or even a delicious cake!" answers Julie as she shows him her basket. "What about you? Did you repair the tractor?" "Yes, but I lost some precious time with this breakdown!" explains the farmer. "You have that much work on the farm?" asks Julie with interest. "Oh yes, I have to feed the cattle and take care of them, cultivate the soil..."

"I can still spare some time, Julie says. "If you want, I can help you. What could I do that would be useful?" "You're very nice, Julie," says Mr. Munch as he walks towards the stable. "Look at good old Bart," he goes on, pointing at his horse. "Could you take care of him? You'd have to bring him some fresh straw and he needs a good grooming. You're not afraid of him, are you?" "Oh no, Mr. Munch!" answers Julie with a smile. "Bart is so nice! Don't worry, I'll take good care of him."

Julie goes up to the horse's stall without hesitation. Bart neighs with joy as he sees her.

The tall horse recognizes the little girl right away. Julie never fails to give him carrots when she walks by his pasture. He sniffs her pockets looking for some goodies while she strokes his neck.

Julie gets a fork from the barn to fetch some fresh straw.
Boy starts running after a cat with a joyful bark. Julie
looks at them: Boy seems to want to play with the cat
who runs away every time the dog gets close. Julie
keeps working because she has no time to waste if she
wants to give her friend Bart a good thorough grooming.

Now Julie takes the currycomb and climbs on
a little stool. Bart is so tall! She starts brushing
his back with all her strength before making his coat
shine. "You'll be as bright as a new pin!" she promises
him. The horse pricks up his ears, as if to show he's
listening to what she says.

Mr. Munch returns to the stable. "You did good, Julie," he says as he sees how well his young apprentice is handling the horse. "You would make a great groom!" Julie is very pleased with the compliment. It is true that 'her' Bart is all spruced up!

"I think it's time for you to go home now," says Mr. Munch. Julie sighs. "Yes. I wish I could stay, but Mommy would worry." She leaves the stable slowly, brushing the straw from her clothes. But where is Boy? It's been a while now since she last saw him. He's probably still busy chasing the barn cat. "I hope he didn't go back to the henhouse," Julie thinks.

Boy comes out suddenly. Julie and Mr. Munch can't help laughing at the sight of him: he's completely covered in straw. He even has some in his ears! "Boy, oh Boy, look at you! You look like a scarecrow!" Julie says laughing. The dog shakes off the straw as his mistress and the farmer watch him.

The time has come to take leave of Mr. Munch. "Here are your eggs," he says, giving Julie a bag. "Free of charge, to thank you for your help. Come back any time you like, you're always welcome. And say hello to your parents for me!" Julie happily heads back home. She can't wait to tell her father and mother how she helped on the farm.